BIANCHI BOOK II

A novel by

Don Bianchi

DEDICATION:

First and foremost I give praises to the most high for making BIANCHI BOOK 2 possible. To my daughter Da'Nasia for helping me make my visions become possible into words. My other daughter Kaziya. I hope when you read this it makes you smile. I love both of y'all pass the moon and back fifty times. This goes for all the hoods in my city. Money Makin' I got it right this time Britt (insider) Accabee (What up Chavis), Rose Mount, The Hike (What up Don Bucks), Bay Side, East and West Side, Back Da Green (What up Suga Don) Wilson St. Pjs, Johnson St. Pjs, Da Rum, Johns Island, James Island, Da Whole We$t Ca$h, Hollywood (What up Skinz) Ravenel, Red Top, Hub Village, South Allen, Rip to Ashley Shores(What up Don Block) Murray Hill, Da Waylyn, East and West Surrey, Horizan Village, Rip George Legre, Liberty Hill, Ferndale, Russell Dale, Liberty Park, 8 Mile, Da whole D Road, Remount Rd (What up Jigga G and Dmoney) 10 Mile, Midland Park (What up Baby Guap and Street Runna), 209, Stall Rd., The Alley, Cross Da Track, I appreciate everyone that supports my BIANCHI brand. RIP RHONDA, MAMA, DADDY, GRANDPARENTS, MARK D, MICKEY JOE, RED, MYRON ,DOLLA BILL, GOAT, COOL C, PICK A BOO, LANDO, LOVER, YAYA, COCO, TOYKA, SPORTY, BIG RUNT, CRIME AND SO MANY MORE I'LL BE HERE FOREVER. FREE LING LING FREE TEKIS. I HOPE YOU ENJOY THIS BOOK BECAUSE IT'S A CLASSIC. BIANCHI FOREVER #HARDERHUSTLE258 #QUIETHUSTLE258

TABLE OF CONTENTS:

Chapter 1: Tangela's Plan

My fingers were quivering as I quickly reached for my phone to dial LJ's number. I always knew having my ears to the streets would pay off in a major way. I became very anxious as the phone continuously rang, and I could barely keep my composure as the seconds went by. The news that I had for him was going to set a lot of life-changing events into motion. Just as I was about to hang up, his deep baritone voice came through my Nokia flip phone.

"LJ, we need to link up ASAP," I said as I flipped my phone shut.

I scurried to my blacked out 1999 BMW 5 Series and raced to one of our usual meet up spots. When I arrived, I circled the block twice and checked my rearview mirrors for anything suspicious just like I was taught by LJ to do. About 10 minutes went by before he pulled up and hopped in my car. We exchanged quick glances, and I started to explain where Procaine and Erica was. I told him I got "word" from an old friend they were in Vegas.

"One of my girls notified me about them checking in at a casino hotel," I began to explain.

I knew my connection was thorough because she was one of the best hustlers I taught the game to! I explained to him we needed to move quickly because I had someone tailing them until we arrived. I wasn't sure where LJ's head was but me and the team were ready to put in serious work. Nothing against my daughter's auntie

Erica, but she was in the way of my money, and nothing comes between me and that paper.

In mid-sentence, he cut me off and said "Tange, it will have to wait until my meeting tonight with Benji and this new connect he found."

Before my brain could think, my lips were already moving. "Let me come with you!! Benji is not made for this business, and I know your entire operation. I already have the girls on standby." "Every decision Benji has made has fucked up our money. With my hustler's instinct, I will have Harder Hustle back up and running in no time."

I could tell I was persuading him to see things my way. To put the icing on the cake, I agreed to be incognito at the meeting and peep the scene only. I wanted to make sure this "Plug" was official because I didn't trust Benji to put his underwear on correctly, let alone run our empire. I also knew this was my foot in the door to Vegas, and I wanted to be in on the action. I needed to prove to LJ that I could run with the best of them.

My only downfall as a hustler was being a female but little do these niggas know, it's actually my greatest asset. He finalized our plans to meet up at the warehouse a little after 5 pm, and then we'll head straight to the airport for Vegas. We exchanged another glance before he dashed off to his home, and I proceeded in the other direction to my own home.

I had a smile plastered on my face, and I was overfilled

with joy. I was thinking about all the moves I was going to make to get us back on our feet. Every single decision Benji made slowed down the team's money, and I would kill him at the speed of light if LJ gave me the head nod. When I walked into my townhouse, I greeted my cousin, hugged, and thanked her for looking after our daughter.

I handed her ten crisp one-hundred-dollar bills and told her I would need her for at least two more days. I skipped up the stairs to my spacious room and headed to my walk-in closet. I felt around the carpet for the trap door I installed. Under the trap door, I kept all my drug money and weapons just in case anything ever went sour. I reached for my BIANCHI MULTICOLORED duffle bag and packed for an overnight stay in Vegas.

With a little over an hour left until the meeting, I went into our daughter Diamanté's room to spend some time with her. Diamanté was the purest version of LJ and I. Her eyes sparkled with innocence, and I always made sure to keep her far away from our street shit. When she gets older, I'll make sure she knows how to protect herself, but for now, all she knows is Mommy and Daddy are bosses of a busy company.

Time flew by and before I knew it, I had to leave. I kissed her on the forehead and gave her a tight bear hug, waved to my cousin goodbye, and rushed out the door. Once I arrived at the warehouse, I did my usual routine and circled the block. I made sure to park on the opposite side of the meet up so I could get a good view of the warehouse and anything pulling in or around the warehouse. Looking through my binoculars, I could tell

LJ was frustrated by how he was pacing back and forth on the phone.

To no surprise, Benji was not there when the "Plug" pulled into the warehouse. As I continued to watch the "Plug" step out his town car, the hairs on the back of my neck stood up. I reached for my cold ass .32 automatic, made sure one was in the chamber, and then took the safety off. Without hesitation, I was trigger ready. I was fuming! The nerve of Benji to have his brother walk into the line of fire alone.

I couldn't believe LJ trusted this clown, family or not. As I watched the exchange, nothing felt right about it. The "Plug" looked more like the white people you see on tv begging for your vote than a hardened criminal with hella weight. Within a few minutes, he handed LJ a heavy black duffle bag and hopped back into his chauffeur driven town car. Just as LJ popped the trunk of his car open, I sprang into action and rushed to him.

My adrenaline was pumping, and I uttered to him "Put the drugs and your gun in my BIANCHI DUFFLE BAG and meet me at the restaurant."

He stared at me for a quick second, and we both uttered in unison "Something ain't right."

I quickly stuffed everything into my BIANCHI bag and handed him the empty black duffle bag. I motioned for him to go before they circled back or something.

My gut had a strong feeling something was "off" about this whole transaction. I needed to be on the safe side because having LJ locked up would be the death to our operation. I climbed into my Beemer and eyeballed the drugs in the bag. From what I could see, it was his colt .45, two bricks of cocaine and lots of money wrapped in rubber bands.

I squealed with excitement and sent a group text to all the Harder Hustle members to meet up at the Spot. I shifted into drive and headed to the red light. Up ahead, I could see the dark sky painted with blue lights. With ease, I turned on an adjacent street where the scene was in my rearview mirror. I wasn't surprised to see LJ was already in the back seat of the squad car, and his trunk was popped open.

I let out the biggest laugh and Harlem shaked all the way to the meet up spot. I knew we were in good hands thanks to my quick thinking. Pulling a boss move like I just did confirmed I was truly ready to put Harder Hustle back on top. I parked my Beemer at the back of Rozay's eatery and walked through the front entrance. The waitress ushered me to the back where his office was located. Rozay's office was soundproof and built to handle Harder Hustle's private meetings.

My best and most trusted three girls Becky, Yazzy, and CeCe were already seated at the long table. Fist walked in not too long after me, and knowing him, he was ready to get down to the nitty gritty. I dropped the duffle bag on the table and quickly told them about LJ. We began discussing what each other's roles were, how to get this weight out on the streets, and what to do with the money that was in the duffle bag. A few hours went by before we were all on the same page about the newly reformed organization.

I would be the head, but Fist also had to give approval on any major decisions. It became clear LJ did not want to be a part of the drug trade, so Fist was the overseer when it came to moving the drugs. We came up with a system to keep checks and balances on all money coming in and going out. No one was above the other, and any money that came in was to be split evenly with each team member.

Rozay was the brain of our operation due to his business mindset. Rozay's entrepreneurship was "unfuckwithable" because he understood everything when it came to business and money. Rozay could clean up anything illegal in a matter of hours. He was a silent partner in a lot of startup companies, and it became the foundation of his millionaire status.Becky, Yazzy, and CeCe were the henchmen. You would be a fool to believe these beautiful women weren't capable of torture and murder. Their loyalty was unquestionable.

Becky was "The Socialite". She was raised in the upper echelon part of Downtown Charleston as Amanda where she developed a talent for robbing the rich. Her family played a part in the gruesome history of slavery. Her grandparents' plantation stood on the grounds of every fallen slave who worked to death picking cotton and taking care of their spoiled asses. Even though she came from a bigot family, she was nothing like them.

Becky hated the upper-class men and took advantage of

every opportunity to rob them. She fit their type to the tee...blonde hair, blue eyes, and the slender frame of a model. It did not take much to lure the men because most of her victims wanted to impress her family or be a part of their riches. Her family had numerous dinner parties, charity events, or a just-because party, and she would pick one random sucker to rob and torture.

Her specialty became throat slitting after she accidentally slit a guy's throat when he tried to tackle her to the floor. She kept a small razorblade underneath her tongue, and she enjoyed the taste of warm blood after each slitting. She never got caught because the police always believed it was a random prostitute setting up old rich white men. With her influence, Becky exposed Harder Hustle to a world they could never tap into on their own.

Yazzy was "The Militant." She enrolled into the Army the very day she turned 18. Her recruiter promised her riches and lavish trips around the world if she signed up. She had a very sheltered life with both parents doing their best to raise her in the church. They protected her from the world, and she was oblivious to the real problems of the universe.

This innocent 18-year-old girl had no idea what she really signed up for. It seemed like blood and carnage was the only thing surrounding her.The putrid smell of blood became so familiar to her and as time passed, she became fascinated with dismemberment and how the body decayed with blood loss. She sat up for hours daydreaming about her kills and if she could beat her kills from the day before.

On a fateful night, she was pulled from her bed and gang raped by her superiors. Yazzy completely zoned out and was fixated on murdering every single one of them slowly. The thoughts of murdering them consumed her so much, she couldn't do her tasks anymore, and her work performance suffered. A month after her traumatic experience, she was discharged from the Army.

With no sense of direction, it wasn't long before she was mixed in with the wrong crowd and was doing murders for hire. Yazzy was soulless and beyond ruthless. She made you want to kill yourself while she was torturing you. She tore your limbs apart slowly and savored the smell of decaying flesh.

Cecilia aka CeCe was "The Fatal Attraction." Unlike the other two women, CeCe was a sweet and gentle woman. She grew up in a traditional Mexican family. Although she was the only child, her parents did everything with her. She cooked with her Mami and danced to salsa with her Papi. A war broke out in her small town, and her parents were killed while protecting their home. Small turf wars seemed to happen on a daily basis, and it was her parents' bad luck to be caught right in the middle of it.

A group of foot soldiers barged in demanding to use their home to stash drugs and guns. When Cecilia's father gave them a stern hard no, they put a bullet through him and his wife's head. At the time CeCe was barely a teenager but her beauty was undeniable. She was all alone. She felt distraught and helpless. CeCe knew she would be overpowered by the soldiers, so she said her

Hail Mary and accepted her fate, but instead of killing her, the foot soldiers kidnapped her and took her to a small village outside of the town she grew up in.

At the village, an elderly lady took her in and taught her how to cook and groomed her to be a housewife so she could marry early. Instead of waiting around for a husband, CeCe lured them to their death with poisonous food. She always chose men who were infamous for being abusive to women. She loved watching them take their last bite of food and realizing it was a woman responsible for their death.

The only team member we were missing at the table was Tiny. Tiny was our go-go gadget recon guy. He became tech savvy after all those years hiding in the woods deep in the country. It was always pitch black, and Tiny had to make sure he saw any dangers coming. He made gadgets out of random things and used them to his advantage to kill or to be his lookout.

We decided the girls would look for Tiny while Me and LJ headed to Sin City. We split the $50,000, and I made sure to put LJ's stacks in the "family" safe for him to get later. The two bricks would just have to wait until we got back. The shop was finally back open and it's time to get back to HARDERHUSTLE258 business!

Chapter 2: Out the Way

While sitting in the back seat of the squad car, I was fuming. My head was spinning with frustration because I had shit to do, and these slimy ass crackas were wasting my time. I was sick of the politics when it came to the drug game. I was sick of the deceit, conniving law enforcement, and ungrateful muthafuckas using me to get over. These dickheads had me handcuffed like a slave, and every second that went by was fueling my rage.

As if these bastards could read my mind, the officer that was driving the limo at the exchange tapped on the window and motioned for me to sit tight. Officer Swenoski aka the "Plug" walked up and announced that he had already called for transport to the County Jail. The "Plug" opened my door and stuck his head in asking if I was enjoying the show.

"In just a minute we gone have the grand finale so sit tight." He said as he chuckled like a lil bitch. He flipped open his phone and began dialing to someone. If only he knew I had front row seats to the biggest drug fail of 2001.

I couldn't wait to see their faces when they realize the bag is empty, and it brought me pure enjoyment. It was almost soothing, and I began to calm down a little knowing the outcome was bad for them and not for me this time. I couldn't wait for them to get the real show started. A few moments went by before two squad cars and the transport van pulled up. Soon after a black limo tinted GMC Yukon with bars on the front grill arrived at the scene.

I could only assume the guy stepping out the Yukon was the "Big Pig" aka Sergeant. On command the officers huddled around him, and Officer Swenoski pointed to the open trunk of my car. The Big Pig motioned one of the officers to grab the bag. I started chuckling to myself when I saw the Officer shaking the empty bag with confusion.

The "Plug" raced to me and began yelling, "Where is it you black bastard."

I replied cockily, "I don't recall why you pulled me over, officer."

His partner quietly asked, "Please tell me you were wearing the wire that I gave you."

The "Plug" dropped his head in disappointment and uttered, "No! I thought we would've caught the piece of shit red headed. His own brother gave us all the intel for goodness sake."

Before I could blink, his partner began hitting him and cursing him out. It took three or four other officers to pull him off Swenoski and break up their fight. "Damn." I said to myself. I was really hoping his partner knocked his ass the fuck out.

In bewilderment, the Big Pig exclaimed "We have nothing…. what the fuck happened here? The city of North Charleston is paying for this bullshit raid, and all we have is an empty bag! What in the holy fuck was supposed to be in the bag?"

Swenoski looked at the ground, kicked at it angrily, and said "fifty thousand cash and two kilograms of cocaine that we took from the evidence room sir."

The Sergeant's eyes grew wide as he spoke through his menacing cold glare and said, "I did not authorize this raid. Wrap this shit up, let him go ASAP, and I'll see you two in my office first thing tomorrow morning."

As the "Plug" began to uncuff me, he muttered "You know we are going to throw the book at your brother, right? We still have him for pending charges, and if you love him, you better cooperate."

I stared at him blankly and responded, "What brother???" I got back in my car and sped off to make up for some of the time I lost.

I dialed Tangela and she picked up on the first ring. Before I could get a word out, she responded "I got everything taken care of...your clothes, the money, the other situation, and the team is all good. I'll fill you in on everything that was said at the meeting on the plane."

"Bet!! Meet me at the airport, and let's get to work," I replied as I U-turned in the direction of the airport.

Back at North Charleston PD, Benny Arnold was relaxing nice and cozy with his feet kicked up on the table in the interrogation room. He was eating a meal fit for a King and loving every minute of it. "I could get used to this shit." He said as he stretched out even further in his chair. His mind started to wander about all the niggas he crossed to get a little piece of money and success.

He could care less about what people thought of him or his respectability in the streets. He thought about the check he was going to cash for snitching and using it as reup money for drugs. This drug bust was a win-win for him no matter what it costed his brother or the relationship his brother thought they had with each other. The sound of the heavy metal door slamming against the wall interrupted his thoughts, and he was manhandled from his chair.

The plate of food he was eating went flying across the room, and the sound of it hitting the floor was deafening. The vice grip he was placed in made him feel weak and helpless. He got choked out to the point that his body went limp; he couldn't think straight and was unable to block the blows he was taking to his body and head. With a blurred vision, he was able to make out the two white men responsible for viciously attacking him.

The "Plug" threw him to the floor while he was being kicked in the stomach and face by another officer he didn't recognize. Officer Swenoski hock spit chewed tobacco on him and yelled, "You are done! Get this good for nothing ass nigger the fuck out of here!"

It was obvious LJ outsmarted them all. The NCPD began a thorough investigation for stolen evidence and both officers were suspended without pay. Benji was convicted for accessory to armed robbery and received a three to six years prison sentence. He became the biggest clown in the Chuck, and everyone laughed and joked about it. The brutal beating he received damaged him so badly he started living in an alternate reality. Benji's' mind and his way of thinking was never the same again.

LJ arrived at the airport in just enough time to board his flight. Tangela was already seated and waiting for him patiently. She glanced at him to make sure he was good and got comfortable in her seat. The three-and-a-half-hour flight from Charleston International Airport to McCarran International Airport was a breeze. By the time their plane landed, LJ was caught up with everything that went down in the meeting. Tangela sent a text "258" to her Vegas source, and they headed to the plane's exit door.

Although it was almost 10 pm, the Vegas sky was lit up and you could see the Vegas strip in the distance. The people were energetic as if it were 10 am instead of 10 pm. They were in awe of the big lights and vibes of the city. It truly looked like a city that never sleeps. Once they grabbed their bags from baggage claim, they headed towards the front door of the airport.

Without a word, Tangela motioned for LJ to get into a navy-blue Toyota Land Cruiser. The driver was a semi heavy-set dark-skinned woman. He could tell by how she was sitting she was thick in all the right places. Tangela hopped in the passenger seat and turned around to make sure he was good. LJ nodded, and they were off to the interstate.

Tangela began small talk with the girl she had nicknamed "Sweetie." She was called Sweetie because she sweet talked the money out of your wallet whether you were male or female.

She began thanking Tangela for everything she taught her. "Vegas got some of the easiest licks girl," she gleamed. "Back in Charleston, you got to do more to get more, but here everybody got it like that. I don't regret leaving one bit, and you should do the same." She said as she panned her eyes to the rear-view mirror and focused in on LJ. "I got every detail about this guy you had me tailing.

"Right now, he's in a luxury suite at the Bellagio. He rents a five-star suite on the 16th floor from time to time, and I confirmed he will be there for the next three days. I recommend catching him in a couple of hours because people in Vegas go to sleep when the sun comes up." LJ nodded his head in understanding and shifted his focus to the neon lights outside of his window.

He wasn't sure if he was going to kick the door down or just wait for this nigga to walk into the suite. All he knew was he had to be very calculated and under the radar. They arrived to a small townhome apartment-styled complex, and Sweetie instructed them to stay in the car. LJ could tell Tangela was also in her thoughts because the only sounds heard was from the engine rumbling.

Sweetie climbed back into the Land Cruiser and passed LJ a Colt .45 semi-automatic. He halfcocked it back to check for a bullet in the head and popped the clip out to check for bullets. She then handed Tangela keys to a rental car placed in a John Doe's name and pointed it out in the parking lot.

As the two got out the car, she said to them "There is a BIANCHI backpack full of all your favorite gadgets and two lightweight bulletproof vests in the backseat of the rental car if you need them. I put three small caliber handguns in the bag, and here is a .40 caliber with four extra clips. Be safe and text me 258 if you need a cleanup." She hugged Tangela tightly and walked off.

They both got into the compact rental with Tangela driving and headed to the Vegas strip. The whole car ride, they plotted an execution plan and an exit route. When they arrived, Tangela circled the gigantic Bellagio Hotel at least six times before LJ felt comfortable enough to walk in without being seen. This casino style hotel was hard to navigate due to the 11 restaurants, casino, spa, five outdoor pools, and five bars it housed besides its hotel rooms.

LJ sat by the bar and picked up on any side conversations pertaining to rooms and how to get around. He overheard a well-dressed older man inviting women to his penthouse style suite. The guy was boasting about only VIP members having access to an elevator that takes them to certain floors. "Bingo!" LJ said as he got up to leave.

He walked up to Tangela, who was blending in at a nearby pool and pretended like he was trying to holla at her. "Meet me at the VIP elevator and bring the swipe card," he said just in case someone might've overheard them. He knew she understood and walked off.

In no time, Tangela headed to the elevator and started panicking. "Oh my god, oh my god!!" She exclaimed, "I can't believe I lost my swipe card." She said this loud enough to catch the same well-dressed man's attention. He was mesmerized by her curves and how her dress clung to her young body.

"I have a VIP key that works on all elevators. I'll give you mine as long as you promise to meet me on the 32nd floor." He grinned. Tangela could barely hold back her laughter.

She couldn't believe this lame ass old man was still using pick-up lines. "I pinky promise," she replied as she exchanged a fake phone number for the VIP key card.

She winked at LJ just as the man walked off to hit on another girl. As the elevator door chimed open, Tangela and LJ hurriedly pressed "16" to get to Procaine's floor. His room was the furthest suite on the floor, but his door stuck out like a sore thumb to them. Tangela quickly opened her BIANCHI bag and grabbed the power drill. She used the silent drill to unscrew the handle from the door. In one swift motion, she took the handle off and eased the door open.

They silently crept into the suite and drew their guns in unison. The air was still, and the suite was silent but the presence of someone else could still be felt. The suite had windows from the ceiling to the floor, and you could see nothing but the Vegas strip and gorgeous skyline. A large couch took up most of the space, and there was only a kitchenette and two doors on the opposite side of the mid-sized room. They shared a quick glance and nodded in understanding to split up and check both doors. LJ took the left, and Tangela had the right.

He could hear her turning the door and when she peeped in, nothing was on the other side except an empty bathroom. LJ silently counted to three as he turned the knob to the master bedroom. As soon as he opened the door, he froze in his step. There was a double barrel sawed off shotgun staring eye to eye with him.

Chapter 3: Dreams Turned to Nightmares

Although the room was extremely dark, their faces were clear as day. Tiny's menacing glare turned into disbelief when he saw LJ and Tangela on the opposite end of his shotgun. "Nigga fuck you doing here," Tiny's deep voice whispered as he lowered his double-barreled shotgun.

"Nigga you know what the fuck I'm doing here, but the real question is why are you here," LJ responded as he lowered and uncocked his firearm.

"Man, everything went left that night in Miami, and I knew I had to answer for that. I had to right my wrongs, and I went into ghost mode tracking down Procaine." Tiny sighed. "I just got in this muthafucka 30 minutes ago. I was waiting for this nigga to come back so I can send him home for all eternity," he said with a snarl.

With Tiny there, they all picked a room to scope and hide out. Tangela noticed a few towels in the bathroom were used, and there were wet spots on the bathroom's marble floor. She checked the bedroom drawers and realized there wasn't any clothes or suitcases laying around. "LJ, I think either they checked out early, or we got the wrong room." She gasped.

"Fuck that; this is the right room," Tiny replied.

LJ had confusion all over his face. He balled up his fist and his whole body got stiff. "You telling me I still can't get to this bitch ass nigga? Tiny get on this shit right

23

now, and Tangela reach out to your people and get eyes on him immediately," he said through clenched teeth. "We back to square fucking one again!"

MEANWHILE....

The morning air was crisp as I stepped down from my private jet and into my chauffeured driven 2001 white on white Lexus LX 470 SUV. This truck wasn't even out yet, and I already had it cruising the Vegas strip. There was something about Vegas that made me feel at home. I could be as flashy as I wanted, and I never felt like I was bringing too much attention to myself.

My life was perfect in this moment. My drug empire practically ran itself; I was making hundreds of thousands of dollars, sometimes millions a day, and I had the love of my life in my arms. Erika completed anything missing out of my life, and I was ready to make her my wife. I was ready to give her the ultimate trophy, Mrs. Procaine, and have her settle down for good.

She had just enough street smarts to be okay if some shit popped off, and her beauty made the world a little less ugly. She was angelic to me, even with her crack cocaine habit. Vegas was going to be our fresh start and where I set up my headquarters for my drug empire.

"Can you see forever and ever til death do us part here baby?" I grinned.

"Yeah, mmhmm," she responded while dozing off.

I could tell her high was coming down, and little did she

know, it would be the last hit I supplied her with. We arrived at the casino hotel, and the bellhops were already outside waiting to unload our luggage. Erika seemed to be in no rush to get to the room. She was like a sinner in hell, and everything she needed was surrounding her. Procaine could tell she was dragging her feet as they got off the elevator to their massive suite.

"Baby, I'mma take a shower, and then we gone continue this conversation about starting a family and making you a housewife," he said as he kissed her softly and headed to the master bathroom.

As the steam began to fill up the bathroom, Procaine felt like he was floating in the room. He was ready to put a baby in her and throw a Royal type of wedding. With nothing but a towel on, he stepped out of the shower and onto the marble floors. "Erika?" he called out with no response. His voice seemed to echo throughout the suite as he looked around for her. It was obvious she had left the room because the door was left wide open. He closed the door, rushed to the master room, and got dressed as fast as he could.

He headed to the slot machines first and scoped the room for her presence. Once he realized she was not in sight, he roamed the hotel and then hit the Vegas strip with no success either. "How far could she have gotten," he murmured to himself. This was Erika's first time in Vegas. She was like an ant in the big city, and no one knew her. As he continued to look around, he felt a wave of emotions. He was angry, disappointed, and concerned about her whereabouts.

He paced their room wondering about where she could be or where she could have gone in so little time. His Lexus was still parked, so he figured she couldn't have gone too far. The constant worry weighed on him so much that he decided to go lay down and think. The oversized analog clock slowly ticked the seconds into hours.

Erika finally stumbled into the room just as the sun began to go down. He jumped up and instantly his worry was replaced with rage and hurt. "Where the fuck did you find drugs so fast and who supplied it to you?" He yelled. For the first time ever, he stared at her and did not see the love of his life. Erika was so high and intoxicated she could barely move.

Procaine underestimated Erika's ability to meet new people. Once she was certain he was in the shower, she stole money out his pocket and snuck out to the hotel's lobby. "Where do you go to have a good time," she said to one of the girls at the front desk. She instructed her to go a couple blocks down the strip to a seedy hotel called the The Desert Mill Motel. This motel wasn't worth one star, even if they paid for it, but to Erika, it was perfect.

She waited around and offered money to everybody she saw for a hit of whatever they had. Erika could care less what she smoked or snorted as long as she got some type of high. Once she ran out of the money she stole, she headed back to the one person she knew would have a lot more...Procaine. Her last hit seemed to kick in just in time because she could see smoke coming from his ears. Her body felt heavy, and everything went dark around her as she collapsed to the floor.

Just like she knew he would, Procaine swiftly picked her up, but instead of gently putting her to bed, he forcibly threw her in the hard bottom tub. The ice-cold water from the shower felt like bullets piercing her skin, and she flinched each time the water splashed her face.

"How could you run out there like that, Erika? I was willing to give you an empire, anything you ever needed, and you would rather be a junky!" Procaine grimaced with tears in his eyes.

He had supplied her habit for years and never realized she was this bad. In that very second, he knew she was going to be his downfall. He loved her entirely too much. She was completely passed out and did not hear him pouring his heart out. His heart shattered and he felt numb on the inside. He called his driver to get their luggage and car ready to go as soon as possible. With no hesitation, he scooped Erika out the shower and headed to the door.

Just as Procaine and the bellhops were going down the elevator, Tiny was on his way up using the stairs. Procaine laid her cold and wet clothed body in the backseat of his car and told his driver to speed to the nearest hospital. Once they arrived, he motioned for his driver to go get a wheelchair and wheel her into the ER waiting room with all her luggage. His heart was beating out of his chest, and he was trying his best to ignore his brain telling him to make sure she was okay.

"Edward, call the pilot and let him know to have the jet ready by 9 pm," he said as his driver headed to McCarran

International Airport. "Vegas will never feel the same," Procaine shrugged as he lit his four-gram high grade marijuana blunt.

He stared at the hospital in the distance and convinced himself Erika was dead to him, whether she lived or not. He boarded his private jet and put all his sadness into his champagne flute.

"Take me to Houston," he directed the pilot as the jet soared at Mach 0.925 through the evening sky.

The three-hour flight was filled with sadness and emptiness. The air felt heavy, and he became very anxious. Procaine swore to himself to never love like that again. He would've left his empire if she had asked him to. The sound of the aircraft's tire screeching the landing strip interrupted his thoughts. William P Hobby Airport was outside his window and the door to the jet was open waiting for his departure.

One of his most prized possession was waiting for him. An all-white Dually Dodge Ram 3500 truck was perfectly parked next to his private jet. The engine hummed louder than the propellers on the jet. The tinted windows were just as black as the tar on the airport's runway. This six-tire big body truck was made for the long haul. He smiled when he noticed his luggage was already loaded into the back of his truck. He climbed into his peanut butter leather seats and drove to a familiar home.

"I'm back Houston," he said as he lit another four-gram

marijuana filled Vanilla Dutch Master.

Chapter 4: H TOWN'S FINEST

As my Dually drifted through the road, I stared at my surroundings and watched the landscape go from rundown ghettos to manicured lawns. "I earned this," I said to myself as I cruised to one of the most prestigious neighborhoods on the outskirts of Houston. Sugarland was one of the best areas to live in. My gated community housed the majority of the "Big Money" in Houston, and I was willing to pay whatever needed to be a part of the community.

Not to get this area of the city confused with the booger sugar I was selling, but Sugarland was heaven to the poorest man. When you turned into his community, you saw nothing but rows and rows of two to three story estates. Each estate had various amounts of acres, and no two homes were alike. I pulled up to my oversized metallic colored electronic gate and pressed "305" to be buzzed in immediately. I drove up a hill to my immaculate ranch style home that was built perfectly on four- and one-half acres of land.

Everything inside of my estate was custom made or imported. Touches of gold were everywhere, and all my cars were parked out front like a display of trophies. I backed my Dually into its normal parking space, and I followed a marble pathway that led to a stable in the backyard. Liberty, my horse whinnied at the feel of my presence. I stroked his midnight-colored mane and proceeded to fill his bucket with water as I fed him a few carrots. I looked in admiration at how well maintained he was in my absence.

I spent well over a $100,000 purchasing this stud, and he has already tripled my profits through breeding and racing. I was tempted to take him for a trot, but I knew I had unfinished business waiting for me inside. I let out a sigh and proceeded through the double door entrance that led to the main entry of my massive home. Specks of gold danced at my feet as I climbed the grand staircase to the room furthest down the long hallway. Without a second thought, I quickly threw my clothes to the floor and wrapped the 500-count silk sheets around my body.

I instantly sank into the plush memory foam mattress as exhaustion set in. Just as I began to lightly snore, the breeze of cold air hit me, and the sounds of the covers colliding with the floor shook me out of my sleep. Standing over my side of the bed was Gisele, my longtime live-in girlfriend that's been with me since high school. The grimace on her face let me know I wasn't getting sleep anytime soon.

"Five months John-Pierre!!" she yelped in frustration.

"You've been away for five fuckin months, and you walk in here like it was yesterday."

"Not this shit again," I mumbled as I picked the covers up and turned over.

She sounded like a broken record, and he was sick of listening to it. He has taken care of her since they were teenagers. Gisele didn't have any hustle to her whatsoever. All the years they were together, she stayed put and brought nothing to the table. Procaine felt like he didn't owe her a damn thing when it came to his business or his whereabouts. He began to doze back to sleep as he tuned out her ranting and pacing back and forth.

"What about our kids?" she spoke, "They barely

recognize you, and I'm losing my mind in this damn house. Between your uncontrollable little brother and the constant needs of your mother, I am overwhelmed. We used to be in this together John-Pierre," she sobbed.

After a brief silence, she realized it was all on deaf ears as he peacefully slept. She climbed in the bed next to him and promised herself to continue the conversation in the morning.

The sun came up quicker than it went down, and Procaine felt well rested. He scanned the room and recalled coming to the one place he did not want to be. He went into his closet and grabbed a robe, silk pajamas, and his Gucci fur slippers. He went to take a quick shower and headed downstairs. His entire family was seated in the dining room while Gisele was frantically cooking breakfast in the kitchen. Mama Pauline looked at Procaine with a twinkle in her eye.

She motioned for him to hug her, and he swiftly ran into her arms. Her motherly embrace felt warm, and even though she couldn't speak, he knew she was happy he was there.

"Everything good with you Ma, you being taken care of?" he asked as she nodded.

"No thanks to you," Baptiste muttered. "You ask the same damn questions every time you bring your ass here. Are you still feeling guilty for mama being in that wheelchair?" he retorted.

Procaine ignored his brother and sat down at the head of the table. There was no use in trying to talk to Baptiste. He was young and didn't understand the streets or what went on in the streets. Baptiste resented Procaine ever since their mother was brutally beaten in a home invasion back in Miami. Since he was always away, some young hitters thought they could torture his family for information on his drugs and money spots. On the night of the invasion, Mama Pauline was alone when they broke in through the window. They pulled her from her bed and beat her for hours until her body eventually gave in, and she had a stroke.

Baptiste came home the next morning and found her in a pool of her own blood unconscious. Instead of wanting revenge, his heart grew in hatred for his older brother and the drug game. Procaine realized years ago he could kill every single one of those niggas' family members, and his brother would still hate him, so he said fuck it. If he got a roof over his head, he'll be alright.

Seeing his mother bound to a wheelchair and not being able to speak hurt him like hell, but he knew she would rather be here because she fought so hard to stay in this world. He paid for round the clock care, and he always made sure she was straight. Anything she wanted or needed, it was a done deal, no questions asked. Houston became the best place for her because it got them far from the city of Miami, and she always loved horses.

The sound of the glass plate hitting the wooden table interrupted his thoughts. Gisele was placing food on the twins' highchair, and he noticed the twins were staring at him blankly. He returned the same blank stare and thought to himself, "Damn, these kids got big, and they are too damn old to be in these highchairs." He shook his head in disapproval and looked down at his plate. The food looked bland and unseasoned.

"I swear this girl can't do anything right," he whispered lowly.

As if Gisele could read his mind, she attempted to give him a kiss as he quickly turned his head and jumped up from his chair.

"I got things to do," he said as she looked with disbelief.

Procaine went back to the master bedroom and changed into his Baby Blue Versace tracksuit and slid his feet into the matching loafers. He made sure to grab the Versace frames and his .44 Bulldog as he went back downstairs and exited the front door. The beams from the sun felt great on his skin, and it shined perfectly on his all white 2001 Ford Excursion. This was the "Money Car" and everyone in the city knew when it was out on the road, that meant it was time for him to collect.

Just like Gisele expected, she grabbed the keys to the Excursion and told him they needed to talk before he leaves. Without a second thought, he ripped his keys from her hand and violently pushed her away from him nearly knocking her down. He wasted no time stepping around her and into his lavish vehicle. "Off to the Bloody Nickel," he said as he blasted his music and sped off to the electronic gate.

The half-hour drive to the best breakfast spot in town felt like torture. He could already taste the pancakes and homemade syrup of Rosie Beez. Rosie Beez was in the heart of Fifth Ward. Fifth Ward was one of the most heavily populated hoods in Houston. Crime was inevitable due to everyone being on top of each other. Most people from Fifth Ward never left because everything they needed was at their doorsteps. When

Procaine pulled into the tiny parking lot of Rosie Beez, he double parked his Excursion and hopped out.

The parking lot was already filled with people chopping it up as they waited for their food or was walking by. The slamming of his truck's heavy door caught everyone's attention, and all side conversations stopped as he walked by. Everyone greeted him, and a few told him they were happy to see him back in the city. He nodded at everyone and walked into the restaurant. He sat in his usual spot as his favorite waitress, Bri, strutted to him with his food already made. A fresh stack of pancakes, scrambled eggs, turkey sausage, warm homemade maple syrup, and OJ with no ice was ready to be digested by him. Bri placed the plate on the table and jumped into his lap.

"I can't wait to see you tonight; you've had me waiting for so long," she said as she fed him his food.

"No doubt," he replied as he tapped her on the butt for her to get up and handed her three crisp one-hundred-dollar bills.

She greeted the next guest and winked at him as she sashayed away. Just as he began to scrape his plate, one of his best workers came through the doors.

The one thing he loved about Fifth Ward was that word spread like wildfire, and his best worker Nickle knew everything going on in the Ward. Nickle was like the mayor of Fifth Ward. He was a certified leader, and he was involved in any and everything that brought money to their poverty-stricken section.

Nickle got his nickname from hustling in Fifth Ward selling fat nickel bags of weed while everyone else was selling a swisher sweet already rolled with weed for you. He grew up in Coke Street Apartments and got it straight up out the mud. Coke Street Apartments was a fenced in project community that had an unguarded tower at the entrance. The ominous projects were overcrowded, and the apartments were stacked like sardines in a can. Crime ran rapid at Coke Street because the cops only came around when someone died or had been shot. Coke Street produced some of the best robbers and hustlers the city had ever known. When Procaine first set up shop in Houston, he heard about Coke Street and knew it would be a money maker for sure.

One day, Procaine parked his car in the parking lot near the Rec Center across from Coke Street and watched with awe as he observed everyone moving around. Anything that could be sold was being sold, and he noticed all the money went to one door. While observing the door, he realized each time someone knocked on the door, it was a young nigga that answered. This young nigga counted the money, and he handed drugs back to whoever knocked at the door. He could tell this lil nigga had his own little operation, and Procaine wanted to infiltrate it by any means necessary.

He came back the next day and knocked on the same door. As he expected the same young nigga answered and said, "Who you looking for?"

"The nigga in charge," Procaine responded as he flashed two birds of cocaine.

"Keep talking," he said as he opened the door for Procaine to come in.

Procaine gave him the run down on how business would

be handled. "I'll bring two birds each time I see you, and I expect $30,000 back."

The young nigga grabbed the birds and told Procaine, "Give me a week."

"Fa sho," Procaine responded and headed back to his car.

The plan was to take over every neighborhood in Houston, and Procaine was starting with Coke Street. This was almost two years ago, and the young nigga Nickle had re upped ten birds faithfully every week since. He dapped Nickle up and motioned for him to sit at the table.

"How's the streets?" he asked.

"Smooth," Nickle replied. "Your truck has already been loaded up with the money I owed you, and my runners already grabbed the birds. We going to need a lot more soon," Nickle said.

"I'll get back to you," Procaine replied as they both walked out the restaurant.

They nodded in unison as Procaine pulled out the parking lot. "This shit is too easy," he thought to himself as he drove to Liberty Rd.

Chapter 5: Nickles and Dimes

Nickle watched in disgust as Procaine's Excursion pulled out of Rosie Beez parking lot. "I'm getting sick of this nigga bird feeding me," he said as he walked into an old ran down abandoned shotgun house in Bucktown where his two main men were waiting for him. Ten birds were not enough to make it through his entire area of Fifth Ward.

 His crew was just starting to get anxious, and Procaine arrived just in time. "This nigga better have some answers soon," Nickle said out loud to himself. He could no longer wait patiently for Procaine to just pop up. Nickle and his small crew were the only ones in the Ward with good coke, and the demand was starting to get too high for the supply Procaine was feeding him.

When he joined his crew inside the rundown shotgun house, he was already prepared to hear them talk shit.

 "Damn ten birds again, huh?" his brother Tru said as he looked through the bag.

"Guess we gone have to put in a little extra work," Bido sighed.

Nickle's crew consisted of him, Tru, and Bido. Bido, was a cousin who grew up in the same household as Nickle and Tru. They treated him more like a brother, and the three young boys were like three peas in a pod. Nickle and Tru came from a two-parent household and were raised to work hard. Their mother worked at the original Frenchy's, a fried chicken restaurant in Third Ward, and their father made a living working at a grocery store called Fiesta.

Their parents' paycheck combined were just enough to pay bills, feed their household, and keep fuel in the only car they owned until their next paycheck. Their parents were so busy working; they were oblivious to who was really moving the drugs in their neighborhood. Nickle saw just how hard they worked for pennies, and he swore to never work for anybody else. The streets of Fifth Ward were all he knew, and it loved him back. When he became a Blood in middle school, it solidified his hood status.

"After we bag up this dope, I gotta play for us," Bido said.

"You know I'm down; fuck what it is," Tru replied.

Out of the three of them, Tru was the youngest and most reckless. Even though he lived reckless, they moved very professionally with any of their side hustles. At night, they broke into establishments to crack into their safes. Bido would peep the location throughout the day to count how many customers came and went. He also made sure no employees went to make a deposit at the bank. Once it was a go they stealthily snuck in, unlocked the safe, and was out before anyone could notice.

Bido was a mastermind. He could crack a safe in his sleep because of how good he was with numbers. They moved so smoothly, these businesses always thought it was an inside job. After the business closed for the day, they snuck in without causing any damage and left no fingerprints. It was the perfect play. The money they made was more than enough to leave Fifth Ward behind, but they loved the hustle. Bido noticed a hustler from the Studewood section of Houston getting heavy foot and car traffic to his restaurant in Acres Homes and came up with their biggest play yet.

"I'm telling y'all we need to hit this nigga when his store is closed, and when he's picking up money from the bank," Bido said.

"So, you wanna jig this nigga?" Nickle questioned.

"Fuck yea, I'm in," Tru said excitedly.

"How you wanna do this?" Nickle asked.

"I say we trail this nigga until we know his routine. He gotta go to the bank eventually. I know this nigga washing that dope money in that bitch. What hood nigga with a business wouldn't?" Bido exclaimed.

"We gotta time this shit perfectly," Nickle responded with seriousness in his tone.

They dapped each other up and finished bagging up the work. At least two weeks went by before they were ready to hit their mark. By the second week, they realized the local hustler usually picked up money from the bank on Mondays and used the cash to re-up his drugs. On Wednesday, he dropped off money to a different bank so they could never be suspicious about his bank transactions. He was the perfect victim because the money they jigged was guaranteed.

Jigging in Texas was a quick come up. Robbers would park their cars not too far from the bank, and they would sit and watch people coming in and out. They waited for someone to come out with an envelope or large bank bag and followed them to their next destination. In most cases, these victims were business owners or errand runners, and they usually had another stop to make somewhere else. The robbers would break into the car and steal the money as soon as their victim wasn't looking.

The local hustler's routine was too predictable. After he picked up money from the bank, he always went to Gessner Ave. to get some pussy from one of his side chicks. He was careless and left the money locked in the glovebox every time. The plan was for the crew to hit the restaurant early in the morning and then him for everything he had. Tru would be outside of the restaurant around 5 am to break in and get whatever he could find in the safe. Nickle would be in the car watching the local hustler at the bank to make sure he picked up the money, and Bido would be waiting around Gessner Ave. for him to go into the apartment.

When Tru got to the restaurant, he crept to the back office and looked around. He checked under the desk for a hidden button, he checked the baseboards for a hidden crawl space, and there wasn't any. He scanned the room and couldn't find any obvious locations for a safe. The walls looked intact, and the small office appeared to be empty. "Where would a hood nigga hide his money?" he thought to himself. A light went off in his head as he rushed to the large walk-in freezer.

The small switch on the opposite wall was begging for him to flip it. As soon as he flipped the switch, a stash spot in the floor opened. "Bing muthafuckin go," he thought to himself as he started stuffing his bag with everything in the hidden safe. He stuffed his backpack full of kilos of coke, pounds of weed, stacks of cash, and a couple of handguns. He moved like a shadow and was out the door before the sun came up at 6 am. Once he was secured, he sent a text to Nickle, "Your turn."

A couple of hours later, Nickle headed to Cadence Bank in Downtown Houston in a stolen 1996 Ford Taurus. Cadence Bank was centrally located and surrounded by high rise buildings. Blending in was going to be easy because in order to get to Cadence, you had to park in a public parking spot and walk to the bank. Nickle paid $7 to park in a private parking lot across from the public parking and watched as the cars were coming in and out. Around 10 am, he spotted the local hustler turning into the public parking in his red 1999 Mercedes Benz E Class.

He was in and out the bank within 20 minutes, and from how he walked and gripped his pocket, you could tell he had money on him. "Go time," Nickle muttered in excitement as he shifted into drive and followed the local hustler to Gessner Ave. The drive to the neighborhood wasn't too far from the bank, so he dialed Bido to let him know to get in position. "Bet," he replied and disconnected the phone.

When the local hustler got to his side chick's apartment, he backed into his parking spot and went upstairs to the second floor of the complex. Once Bido saw him walk through the door, he slowly crept to the Mercedes passenger side door. Just as he got to the door, Nickle parked three parking spots down to make sure he got a good view of the apartment door the hustler went into. Bido used a small pocketknife and bobby pin to open the glove box. It popped open with ease, and he grabbed the overfilled bank bag and crept towards Nickle's car.

The local hustler came flying down the stairs and whipped out his automatic. Before Bido could make it to the car, the hustler had already started firing shots. As bullets rang out, one pierced Bido's chest, and he fell back into the Ford Taurus door. Nickle rushed out the car and fired two shots at the local hustler. Both bullets penetrated his head and chest as he dropped to the ground.

Nickle quickly dragged Bido to the car and put him in the backseat. He frantically sped off towards Memorial Hermann Hospital. "Cuz stay up man, we go be to the hospital in a sec man just stay up please cuz," Nickle said as he bobbed and weaved through the busy 610 Houston traffic.

Bido shared a glance with Nickle through the rearview and nodded off as soon as their eyes locked. Nickle banged the steering wheel until both his hands went numb.

"Aye bro, meet up with me by Rosie Beez," Nickle said as soon as Tru picked up. When he pulled into the parking lot of Memorial Hermann, he parked and prepared himself. As much as it hurt to leave his cousin, he knew he had to go and fast. He wiped everything down and grabbed the bloodied bag from the grips of Bido cold hands.

"My brother for life," Nickle said as he left and jumped on the Metro bus headed to Rosie Beez.

The 30-minute bus ride and five-minute walk to the restaurant was nothing to Nickle, but his feet felt heavy with every step he took. Tru was already in the parking lot when Nickle finally arrived.

"He gone," Nickle whispered in disbelief as his body dropped to the ground.

"Fuuucccck," Tru said as he helped his brother get up off the ground.

"Did you get that nigga?" He asked.

"You already know," Nickle responded.

"Well then we did right by big cuz!" Tru said with relief.

"Let's go count these bricks, pounds, and money," he said to try and ease their minds.

It took them almost three hours to sort through the drugs and money. There was over $170,000 cash and at least 15- and one-half kilo of cocaine and more than 25 pounds of weed.

"What's next big bro?" Tru asked as he stared at all the weight they had.

"I'm coming up with a new game plan now lil bro," Nickle said as he shook his head with tears in his eyes for Bido.

Chapter 6: The Exterminator

Meanwhile back in Vegas, LJ's patience was wearing thin as the minutes went by without any results on Procaine's whereabouts.

"We need to get the fuck up outta here," he yelled out.

"The next flight is in an hour," Tangela murmured as she went over to him and gave him a hug.

"Everybody will be on top of it as soon as we touch down in the Chuck," she whispered in his ear to reassure him.

The flight back to Charleston was more silent than usual as the three of them thought about another way of getting at Procaine. It seemed like their window of opportunity was closing, and this nigga was becoming more impossible to get to as the days went by. When they landed, Fist was parked out front in a Lincoln Navigator waiting for them.

"Y'all boy good?" he asked in his thick Geechie accent as he gave LJ his pistol. He could see the puzzled looks on their faces.

"I need this shit over with," LJ responded with his lip twisted up.

"I got some other shit for you," Fist, replied as he pulled out the airport's parking section.

"Wa you got bubba?" LJ said in Geechie with a blank stare.

"I got your boy Dazzle in a grip, and we gone go handle that as soon as we drop off Tangela and Tiny. You can take some of your frustration out on that nigga," Fist chuckled.

"Yeah, that snitch nigga gotta leave here pronto," LJ responded as his face started to brighten up at the thought of finally getting his hands on Dazzle.

"If y'all need extra help, let me know," Tangela mentioned from the backseat ready to put in work as usual.

"Y'all two stay on top of this Procaine shit; me and Fist gone send Dazzle to meet up with his maker," LJ replied.

Once Tiny and Tangela made it to her car at Rozay's restaurant, they went into go mode. Tiny rented a car and went to the only place he knew, which was Eutawville. Eutawville was a very small country-like city on the outskirts of Charleston. Eutawville was surrounded by trees, and it had a jungle-like feel to it. Tiny knew those woods like the back of his hands, and he also knew where to hide a body for the wolves or coyotes to find you and never be seen again. Since Eutawville was outside of Charleston, all his connects to the streets were small time local hustlers. His chances of getting information on a big fish like Procaine was slim, but he knew it was worth a try. When he pulled up to a rundown cottage on Gillens Rd, he saw nothing but live action. The dope boys were inside cooking up, and the junkies were coming and going. To the average eye, it looked like a cookout going on but Tiny knew what was really going down.

"Aye, where Billie Dee at?" he asked a junky that was about to light up his crack pipe.

"He in the back youngin." The junkie sniffled.

Tiny went up the uneven stairs and into the small but crowded cottage. BD short for Billie Dee was the head honcho in Eutawville. He ran the area, and all the wannabe dope boys looked up to him. If anybody had information, he was the person that would know or could find out.

"Aye bruh, I need you to tap into the streets and get me some info," Tiny said as soon as he laid eyes on BD.

"You know I gotchu, but my reach ain't bout so far. I'ma need some time," he responded.

"I gotta bag for you and your people if you can get that," Tiny insisted as he began to give him the rundown on Procaine.

"I'll hit you," BD said as he dapped up Tiny.

Tiny left knowing he set the bait, and he was just waiting for the fish to come biting. While Tiny and Tangela was trying to get some kind of information, Fist and LJ began to circle the block where Dazzle lived. Dazzle been on the hit list for snitching, but LJ felt like he had bigger problems to worry about. He thought the streets would've handled him by now, but the street code on snitching wasn't the same anymore.

Back in the day, you couldn't be seen anywhere once you snitched or even being seen hanging with a snitch. Nowadays, niggas will get locked up with a book full of charges and be home before they even made it to bond court. Snitches used to play it off like "man they fuck up my paperwork," but now them niggas be like "as long as I still got the drugs and money, niggas gone fuck with me." Dazzle was the slimiest because he was smiling and living it up like life was sugarcane sweet. He had to go today for sure, and that's on Meano!

When they pulled up to his street named Jacksonville Rd, there was one row of five houses on each side. The road was so narrow, you could see from the head of the road. Dazzle's car was not in his driveway, but Fist circled around just in case. The house looked unoccupied, so it was obvious he wasn't home.

"This nigga name ain't Dazzle for no fuckin' reason bra. I know where this flam ass nigga at," Fist said as he drove to the only other place he could be.

Dazzle was a social type of dude and stayed in ODC. ODC was a small social club on Dorchester Rd. about five minutes away from his home.

"Two in the afternoon, and this nigga in the club," LJ murmured as he shook his head at the sight of Dazzle's car in the parking lot.

Fist pulled into the Hess gas station across from the social club to wait for him to come out. Before he could shift his SUV into park, Dazzle stumbled out and hopped into his Range Rover.

"How you wanna do this?" Fist glanced over to LJ.

"Follow his ass home. We gone take our time killing this clown." LJ fumed with rage filling his soul as he grabbed the duct tape out of the glove compartment.

As soon as Dazzle pulled up to the intersection, Fist was on his tail. As they got to the next light, Dazzle made a right and turned onto another street. Realizing the car behind him made the same turn, he began to feel uneasy. He didn't know if the combination of liquor and weed laced with coke had him paranoid or if the car was really tailing him. He mashed the gas and swiftly turned onto Accabee Rd. His heart dropped as he watched the black

Lincoln do the same thing.

Up ahead, the red warning lights flashed in the sky to signal an oncoming train. Dazzle knew it was impossible to U-turn on this small road without colliding with the wide body SUV. As he prepared to stop at the railroad tracks, he knew hopping out was his only option.

"Got his ass," LJ chuckled at the circumstances.

Dazzle was stuck and he knew it. LJ clutched his pistol and downed his window making sure the safety was off. Just as he aimed, Dazzle flew out his car and onto the train tracks.

"Where this nigga think he going?" Fist huffed at the thought of chasing behind this jokey ass nigga.

Before Dazzle could plant both feet on the ground, the train crashed into his body and sent him flying into final eternity. A minute or so later, the red lights stopped blinking, and Dazzle's mangled body laid in the distance.

"Damn, why can't all snitches go out like this?" LJ said laughing for the first time in years. Fist shook his head and drove around Dazzle's abandoned Range Rover.

Tangela knew if anyone could locate Procaine, it would be her. She done it once, and she could do it again. She pulled up on CeCe, Yazzy, and Becky to fill them in on Vegas.

"This shit is crucial now. We need all eyes on this nigga," she spoke.

"I gotta plan, but it's risky as fuck," CeCe mentioned with uncertainty in her voice. "I can get his whereabouts, and every little detail about him, but if we do this shit, we will owe some heavy hitters. Once we in, ain't no out with these muthafuckas." She began to explain.

"If that's the case, let's run it by the whole team." Tangela sighed as she began to dial LJ.

The crew met up at Rozay's restaurant at 6 pm sharp. They all went to the back, and CeCe went to the head of the table.

"I'mma be real with y'all. I got blood ties to a Mexican cartel named The Riviera Cartel. This ain't just any ol' cartel either. My family has been running shit for over 100 years. They are very traditional and only fuck with their kind. I remember my mami talking about the power they had and how much she feared them. She distanced herself from them because she chose to marry outside of the cartel."

"My family is so ruthless anybody that goes against the grain will lose protection, and they will spread the word." She continued. "If you aren't killed by someone else, they will find you and kill you themselves. When my mami was killed, she was already labeled as a traitor. My blood ties give me access to them, but once they do us this favor, we will owe them for life," she admitted.

"I ain't with that owing shit, but I ain't against the plan to use them for information...anybody got another solution?" LJ questioned.

"It's going to take my people a minute, so I'm going where y'all going," Tiny shrugged.

"This could be a new connect opportunity," Tangela squealed in excitement. "This could extend our reach also. We could have the whole state on lock, especially once we get Procaine out the way," she said trying to persuade everybody else.

"If that's the case, I can open a second restaurant and some new business venture for the team," Rozay pondered as he started plotting their money moves.

"We go where the money go, ain't that right Becky?" Yazzy said as she dapped up Becky.

"Y'all know I don't want shit to do with drugs. If this is what y'all wanna do, I'm all for it. I just want Harder Hustle to be unstoppable...Fuck em; we cross that bridge when we get there about that owing shit," LJ confirmed as he looked everyone in their eyes.

"So, where we going then?" Becky asked excitedly.

"Muthafuckin San Antonio Tx," CeCe chimed.

Chapter 7: The Ranch

CeCe fingers trembled as she dialed a number she never thought she would ever use. "Only in a life-or-death situation, hija." Her mami would always say as she made CeCe recite the phone number to her repeatedly. To CeCe, remembering her grandfather's phone number was like remembering your social security number. Rodrigo Riviera answered on the third ring, and his ominous voice sent a shiver down her spine.

"Hola Abuelito," CeCe said as she tried to elude confidence in her voice.

Rodrigo knew immediately it was his estranged granddaughter "Cecelita" calling because only close family members had his direct phone number.

Rodrigo Tomas Riviera was a traditional Mexican man. He was so old that his age became a mystery. He seemed immortal, and his reputation was well respected in Mexico and in the United States. His rage could fill a room without speaking, and from his presence, you knew he demanded respect. He was so traditional, he rejected and outcasted his only daughter for marrying outside of their family's cartel.

It was no secret to them both he could have cared less about Cecelita, but being traditional means that blood made her connected to the cartel.

"Habla Alto!" He grumbled back to her.

On command, she raised her tone and told her grandfather what she needed. "Go to San Antonio and see your Tio," he said in very badly spoken English as he immediately disconnected the call without saying another word.

CeCe's heart jumped out her back at the sound of the dial tone, and she felt lost. She wasn't sure if he gave her his blessing or not, but one thing she knew for sure was to not call him back. She was potentially walking the whole Harder Hustle Crew into a line of fire but what other choice did they have? Her mother always told her stories about the family's ranch in San Antonio. She felt her mother's presence in that moment and knew the crew had an angel looking out for them.

The entire flight to San Antonio was like deja vu. Visiting a place she never been to before, but she knows every detail about it felt eerie to her. The ranch was almost two hours away from the city life of San Antonio. The road went on for miles with nothing but trees in sight. At the end of the road was a massive gate with Riviera engraved on it. The heavily armed guards glanced into their truck and proceeded to open the gate.

The ranch looked exactly like CeCe's mother described. There seemed to be hundreds of acres of land with a ranch style mansion centered by a lot of smaller homes. The ranch looked like its own busy city. Cows, chicken, pigs, and other wildlife roamed freely. Women and children seemed to be doing domestic task like cooking, cleaning, and gardening. There was a school on site and a slaughterhouse nearby. They also had two man-made lakes bordering around the entire property.

The ranch was ran like a tyranny. Women and children were not allowed to leave the ranch at all. Men who were assigned to leave were allowed to gather necessities the ranch could not produce and come back immediately. When the crew pulled up to the mansion, a slender Mexican man stepped out of the immaculate palace with four guards surrounding him. CeCe could tell based on her mother's description of her uncle Emilio he was standing before her.

"Cecelita," he said with a serious tone. "These guards will escort you to the grand room."

Emilio Tomas Riviera was the poster child for flunkies. After witnessing the consequences his older sister endured for going against his father wishes, he did everything that was asked of him whether he agreed with it or not.

"Miguel show Cecelita's guests around," he said as he prompted another guard to the crew.

All the Harder Hustle members glanced at CeCe to make sure she was going to be okay. After a subtle nod, they parted ways as CeCe walked into the mansion with the three other guards. Two guards proceeded to open the double doors to the grand room. The last guard blocked the entrance to the room once they were inside. Each guard inside stood next to the door and waited on standby.

CeCe did not know whether to sit or stand, and for the first time in her life, she felt intimidated. After two small knocks, the door was opened, and Emilio walked in and asked,

"You finally need la' Familia like padre said you would?" His loud voice bellowed through the great room.

"Yes Tio," CeCe responded. "There is a narco named Procaine, and we need him out our way. His existence will always threaten our organization."

"Hmmm." Was her uncle's response as he seemed

unimpressed by the favor she was asking for.

"This narco means so much to you that you are willing to be indebted to us?" he quizzed.

"The benefits outweigh the debt," she replied. "We are willing to pay whatever for this information."

"Fair enough, get comfortable," he retorted as he walked out of the grand room.

He directed the guard to bring his satellite phone so he could make a clear call to his father. After explaining CeCe's need in detail, his father requested he keep the crew overnight and give them the information in the morning. The Riviera Cartel had plans to milk the Harder Hustle crew dry and whether CeCe knew it or not, she was going to pay for every bad decision her mother made.

Emilio stepped back into the grand room and told her to join her crew outside. "I'll have everything you need in the morning," he said as he ushered her away.

The crew stared in awe as they were escorted around the ranch. Tangela was the most impressed, and she did not care to hide it. She really hoped CeCe's family welcomed them into their organization because having connections in Mexico was like striking oil. She could tell they were highly organized and precise. She saw the ranch more like a business instead of a village. There were trucks coming in and out, and everybody seemed to be doing their part to keep the ranch running smoothly. As a Queen Pin in the making, she wanted to learn as much as she could.

The guard took them to a small Mexican style home near the mansion and told them this is where they will be staying. The small home had a cozy feeling, and it reminded CeCe of a traditional Mexican home.

"Dinner is soon, and attendance is expected," the guard said before he walked off.

"Wassup CeCe, you got what we need?" Tangela asked wasting no time."

"Not yet." CeCe sighed as she sunk into the small tattered couch. "We gone get the info in the morning, so everybody lay low until then. I'mma be real with y'all once my uncle gives us this info; we gotta be ready for whatever," she said with a concerned look.

"Fa sho," Tangela said as she glanced over to LJ who seemed to be in a deep thought.

The sound of a large bell interrupted his thoughts quickly, and the crew headed outside. The entire village was walking towards a building near the back of the mansion. The room had rows of tables lined up, and the aroma of food overtook their noses. Fruits and vegetables were stacked high in baskets. Any animal you could think of was being served buffet style. The people of the ranch came alive as they ate and danced to the music, and the strong smell of marijuana was everywhere. The crew were treated like VIPs, and Tangela loved every minute of it.

At the end of dinner, Emilio announced curfew will be at 8 pm and anybody out after that will be shot on site. The crew wasted no time getting back to their temporary housing. They stayed up all night contemplating how they could make sure the debt benefited them.

"Worst case scenario, we shoot it out," Tiny shrugged.

"I say we break bread; we ain't no slaves and we ain't working for free. We should pay whatever they ask for product," Tangela gleamed.

"Y'all can have that drugs bull shit. I want to get to Procaine and worry about all that other shit later," LJ said.

"Agreed," CeCe replied as she let out a yawn. She wasn't sure if the flight had her exhausted or the constant anxiety she felt from being on the ranch. Once she showered and laid into the bed, her body drifted into a deep sleep.

The feeling of a dark presence shook her out her sleep, and she woke up to her uncle standing over her. "Get your guests together, and meet me in the grand room," he said as he walked into the darkness.

CeCe did a quick glance at a small digital clock and realized it was only 3 am. She shook everyone out their sleep, and they all walked over to the mansion. The same guards opened the double doors and instructed them to have a seat. Emilio was already seated inside. He was extremely hard to read, and CeCe's stomach sunk with every second that went by.

"Cecelita, this narco that you mentioned is here in Texas....Houston actually," he said as he motioned the guard to give her a piece of paper with all his information.

On the paper was his address, his license plates, and a description of all his cars. "Now that you've agreed to be indebted to us, you have the Cartel's permission to kill him."

"Permission?" CeCe pondered.

"Sí, you see this narcotraficante is in our network; killing him would mean less money for our organization. Why would we want that? You're going to replace him and handle his load plus double," he said with a slight grin.

CeCe's heart sank as she realized there was no way out once they started selling for her family. "There has to be another way," she mumbled in disbelief.

"Afraid not," he said as he instructed the guards to escort them out to their vehicle that was already parked out front. "I look forward to doing business with your crew, and I'll be seeing you soon sobrina," he said with a sinister glare.

Fist began to drive off as CeCe stared out the window in a deep trance. Was this how her mother felt when she left the ranch and went back to Mexico? She felt stuck, her mind was racing, and her heart was beating out of her chest.

"What's so wrong with doing business with your family?" Becky asked.

"It seems like a win-win situation for us," Tangela added.

"Once they own us, they can control us," CeCe gasped. "Remember when I said be ready for whatever? This is the whatever," she said as they headed to Houston.

Chapter 8: The Infrastructure

Touching down in Houston felt surreal to LJ. The air felt different, and he could feel a weird presence surrounding him. He couldn't figure out the presence, but he also didn't think too much about it. LJ could give two fucks about how their trip ended, just as long as he was able to kill Procaine. He was tired of the back-and-forth cat and mouse game they were playing.

"No matter what, this nigga got to die! I won't accept no failures from anyone this time," he said as everyone nodded with understanding.

To the team, this was business, but for LJ this was beyond personal. Avenging his unborn son, his one and only love Sasha, and his best friend Meano was his primary goal in life, and it was going to get done by any and all means necessary.

"I got somebody who gone hook us up," Rozay said as he interrupted LJ's thoughts. "My boy Marcus has been rocking with me since the days of being on the block hustlin'. He gone get us straight while we down here with anything we need," he said reassuringly.

Rozay began dialing Marcus, and when he answered, he gave Rozay the address to his restaurant called Fowlers in Midtown. Midtown Houston was an extension of Downtown, and it was infamous for its restaurants and nightlife. It was in the middle of all the action and the perfect money-making location for any business. It did not take the team a long time to arrive to Fowlers. Fowlers was a small brick building with an upscale rooftop bar.

Although it was a small restaurant, the rooftop overlooked the city, and the vibes alone brought hundreds of customers. Marcus dapped Rozay up and showed them around the restaurant. He wore a tailored suit, and his Cartier frames and matching watch solidified his expensive taste in clothing. Marcus looked like a businessman, but a real street nigga recognized another one when they saw him. Rozay and Marcus grew up in the trenches of Philly together.

Even though Rozay was a couple of years older than him, they both looked up to each other as equals. They both had the same goal, to get the fuck outta Philly, and leave the grimy shit alone. The only difference was Rozay didn't mind getting his hands dirty from time to time. Marcus and Rozay touched a lot of money together, and whatever one learned, they made sure the other one learned too. After the tour, Marcus sat the Harder Hustle team down and instructed one of his hostesses to bring them whatever they wanted.

"Lunch on me," he said as he turned to Rozay. "While your team is in town, I got you... whatever you need!" he said with pride.

"Yeah, we gone need a spot to lay low and a lot of equipment for our stay," Rozay expressed.

"I got a rental property 15 minutes away from here on

Westheimer in the Galleria area. This is the address. I'll have my boy Mickey Joe stop by with the equipment," Marcus said as he began writing the address down on a piece of paper.

"Fasho!" Rozay confirmed as he handed Marcus $10,000 in stacks of one-hundred-dollar bills.

"Enjoy y'all meal, Ima head out to a meeting," Marcus hurriedly stated as he pocketed the money and left the restaurant.

After they all ate, they traveled to the condo on Westheimer. Westheimer was the home of luxury. It was surrounded by high rises and the world-famous Houston Galleria Mall. Westheimer was the Rodeo Dr of Houston. Their condo was in the middle of Westheimer, right off Interstate 610, but it still had a duck off feeling to it. They felt like they were hiding in plain sight.

Once they were settled in, the team sat on a long sectional and had a meeting about their execution plan. "How y'all wanna do this?" Fist asked starting the meeting.

"We gonna take over this nigga operation, so I say we study this nigga for a couple of days with the information we already got on him," Tangela exclaimed convincing everyone else.

"While y'all doing that, Tiny and I finna scope this nigga house out. He brought it to my doorstep, so I'mma bring it to his," LJ said with a grimace.

"After a day or two, we will figure out how to execute this nigga and take over his spots." Yazzy smiled as she began to think about how she was going to torture Procaine.

In the middle of the meeting, the doorbell echoed throughout the condo, and Rozay got up to answer the door. "This is Marcus's boy, Mickey Joe; he got everything we need," he said as he introduced Mickey Joe to the crew.

Mickey Joe dropped a large duffle bag and suitcase on the counter, and Yazzy's eyes lit up. The duffle bag had a bullet proof vests for everyone, pistols, extra clips with bullets, and even a few hand grenades. "Holla if y'all need something else," he said in a deep southern Texan accent as he left the condo just as fast as he came.

"This country ass nigga got us right," Fist exclaimed.

"We ready for whatever," Yazzy said in agreement with Fist.

"The Cartel said this nigga got at least four dope spots in Houston. We should team up just in case some shit goes sour," Becky mumbled.

"That's a bet!" CeCe said as she began loading bullets into the clips of the pistols.

Once they all split up into teams of two, they rented several vehicles under Rozay's many LLCs. LJ and Tiny sat outside of the estate for hours waiting for Procaine to come home. They didn't see any maid services or gardeners coming to enter a code at the gate. The home seemed silent and still. LJ nor Tiny could see beyond the gate, but they knew they were in the right spot.

"We gone have to hit this nigga another way," he said to Tiny.

Meanwhile CeCe and Becky started scoping out the dope house in South Park. CeCe could tell these niggas were cut from a different cloth. They operated like they were for themselves. Some workers were taking lots of shorts, selling the work, and other workers were giving away too much product for less money. CeCe could also tell the South Park niggas were going to be a problem. They were loud, rowdy, and too reckless.

"Who gone keep these niggas in line?" Becky questioned.

Fist and Tangela picked Liberty Rd. where Procaine had two dope houses because of how big the area was. Tangela's eyes lit up as she watched the "money" coming and going. There was a corner boy everywhere you looked, and it was obvious Procaine had taken the section over with ease. Both trap spots were booming. Niggas and fiends came in and out like clockwork.

"We gone have to make sure these niggas know who the boss is around this muthafucka," Tangela huffed to Fist as she passed him the blunt.

"Yeah, the last thing we need is a turf war fucking up our

money," Fist said quickly in agreement.

Although Rozay knew the mission, his primary goal was to find a new business venture lucrative enough to wash the money they would be bringing in from Procaine's operation. He researched tirelessly and decided to sit down with Marcus again to see where the money is in Houston. He wanted to make sure they had a business set up before their first shipment came in from the cartel in less than a week.

Yazzy wasn't worried about being alone scoping out Fifth Ward. From what she could see, this operation was much smaller. She observed only one or two niggas at the most with coke. Yazzy admired the young hustler as he moved solo. He exchanged the coke and collected his money with ease. He was hard to read, but she could tell he was all about his hustle. From what she could see, anyone that walked up to him came with respect and showed him much love.

"He gone be a perfect fit." She thought to herself as she texted the group "GOOD TO GO" and sped off. Yazzy felt like she didn't need to scope any longer. She had a gut feeling about the worker in Fifth Ward, and the team was going to put him to the test. A few days passed before the crew felt comfortable enough about infiltrating Procaine's operation. CeCe and Becky voiced their concerns about the South Park niggas.

"Who gone stay back and babysit this operation?" Becky asked with concern.

"No need," Yazzy nodded. "I got a problem solver. There is a little nigga in Fifth Ward running the whole area alone. I think he has a Harder Hustle mentality. I say we test the lil muthafucka's loyalty to Procaine and see if we can bring him onboard. If he a real nigga like I think he is, then we can give the operation to him. He is from here, so it's a win-win for us," she suggested.

"If he ain't down, we gone remove his ass. It's that simple," Tangela shrugged in agreement.

"Well then, let's load up and head out to Fifth Ward," CeCe gleamed as she passed Tangela a Tec .9.

"It's time to make some noise" Yazzy said as she cocked her pistol.

"While the girls head out to Fifth Ward, Fist get eyes on Procaine, and tail the nigga as much as possible. We need to know his every move. Tiny and I gonna sit back outside his house to get the code or see anything coming and going," LJ said with excitement realizing their plan was coming together perfectly.

"In the meantime, I'mma go sit down with Marcus; we need to have a business set up before the first big shipment come in from the Riviera Cartel," Rozay said.

Everybody got up to leave, and LJ felt the rush of adrenaline through his veins. Harder Hustle was about to take over Houston, and no one will be able to see it coming until it's already done.

Chapter 9: When the Smoke Clears

Part One:

Tangela felt superior as she gripped her tech 9. She was ready to put holes in this nigga if he didn't cooperate. Finding him was too easy, and it made her trigger finger itch.

"Ayo Papi...where can me and my chicas find weed at round here," CeCe yelled out her window to Nickle.

"I got what y'all need," he responded as he glanced into the small car filled with four beautiful women.

He instructed the girls to drive into Coke Street Apartments and meet him at apartment 1710. Becky, Yazzy, CeCe, and Tangela looked more like around the way girls instead of ruthless serial killers.

Once they were inside the small apartment, Becky whipped out her pistol and pointed it at Nickle.

"Sit yo ass the fuck down!" she demanded.

Nickle sat down with ease as he made a bird call noise. Yazzy cocked her pistol and pointed it at him also.

"I dare you to make another sound," she said while sliding Becky to the side.

Seconds later, she felt cold metal on her temple. "You bitches need to come correct," Tru said.

"We ain't no sucka ass niggas, ain't no hood hoes robbing us today," he barked as he scanned the room.

"Well, I guess this ain't gone end well for y'all," CeCe sighed as she pointed both of her pistols at Nickle and Tru. If they blinked for even a second, she was head shottin' them both.

"We all got off on the wrong foot," Tangela said to Nickle with a smile. "Let's all drop the guns and talk business," she suggested.

"Nah y'all first," he replied as Tangela motioned for the girls to lower their guns.

"What kind of business we need to be talking?" he asked blankly.

Tangela pulled out a chair next to him and began rolling a blunt. "We taking over Houston and we gone need runners." She said as she began passing around the first blunt.

"I don't run for nobody," Nickle said as he and his brother both refused the blunt. For all they knew, these bitches were looney as fuck and laced the blunt.

"Name your price then. We willing to pay whatever," Yazzy said as she interrupted Nickle.

"Nah I'm good," Nickle replied as he brushed her off.

"Did you know Procaine got three other dope spots?" Tangela asked as she took long pulls of the weed.

"Each of these other spots are getting thirty birds or more a week. Go to South Park or Liberty Rd and see how them niggas getting down, especially Liberty Rd. All y'all niggas got the same connect. We offering you all their areas plus more. We tryna put the right person in this position that deserves it." She looked him dead in the eyes as she got up from her chair.

"Think about your price, then meet us here and don't take too long to decide," she said as she wrote down the condo's address and left out the door with the girls.

"Who is these go-go gadget ass bitches?" Tru asked as he couldn't believe he was about to shoot it out with some beautiful hoes. "These bitches living it up on Westheimer. Who the fuck these bitches working for?" he thought to himself out loud as he looked over the address.

"I don't know, but fool I can't believe this nigga Procaine been disrespecting us like that, and how the fuck do these hoes know we moving work for this nigga?" Nickle said through clenched teeth.

"I been asking this nigga for more birds for the longest, and he been acting tongue tied like he ain't got it. We going to this meeting, and then I'm murdering that nigga!" he said menacingly.

"You really think we can trust these bitches?" Tru asked in astonishment.

"We gone let them put their cards on the table. Either way, I'm deading Procaine. If they willing to give us whatever we ask for, then they gotta mean business," Nickle said convincing his brother.

"I'm down big bro, I'd hate to shoot up Westheimer but fuck it; let's see what these bitches talking," Tru responded as they walked out to Nickle's '79 Burgundy over Grey candy painted Convertible Cadillac Eldorado.

Everybody in Fifth Ward knew it was a special occasion when Nickle pulled out his candy painted Caddy with the '84s spoked rims and vogue tires. The leather interior looked like peanut butter with the wood steering wheel complimenting it perfectly. When he popped the trunk, THE WORLD IS YOURS NICKLE was lit up in neon lights. Nickle was riding through the city on suicides. Back then, driving the type of car Nickle had would be like committing suicide because everybody would try to rob or kill you for your car, but mostly for the rims aka swingers. His hood status was certified, and Nickle was always strapped, so he wasn't worried a bit.

The entire 25-minute ride, Nickle weighed out his options in his head. He was going to fuck with the girls until he felt like he couldn't trust them anymore. When he pulled up to the condo, he knew they were touching real big money. He could hear the doorbell ring from outside, and he automatically clutched his pistol.

"Good...you didn't take too long," Yazzy said as she opened the door wide for him and Tru to walk in.

"The whole team is waiting in the living room," she said as she instructed them to follow her.

Nickle felt outnumbered and shared an uneasy glance to Tru. Tru was intrigued, and he knew he was dealing with the best of the best. He stared back at Nickle and nodded in approval. As soon as Nickle sat down, he looked everyone in their eyes, and they all looked directly at him. He felt respected and relaxed a little bit off his pistol.

"I'm going to accept y'all offer, but I want eighty keys, on top of all the dope spots, and I want to pick my runners. I ain't willing to share my plate with Procaine either. No disrespect but I'mma kill that nigga for fucking with my money," Nickle said lowly.

"What's your name?" LJ asked.

"Nickle," he responded.

"What you got in mind with Procaine?" LJ questioned.

"I'm meeting this nigga tomorrow for ten damn birds at this restaurant in Fifth Ward named Rosie Beez. He usually leaves his truck unlocked for me to load up the re up money and grab the work, or I walk into the restaurant to get the duffle bag filled with dope. I was going to off him in the parking lot or follow him home depending on how he set up the drop," Nickle shrugged.

"Let us handle that part; we got a shipment coming in two days. After the drop, you can have all the bricks you need," Tangela replied to Nickle.

"That's a bet then," Nickle said as he looked around the room at the crew he'll be doing business with.

"If you good to us, then we good to you." Yazzy smiled as she passed Nickle a BIANCHI BACKPACK filled with $100,000.

"Welcome to Harder Hustle," the team said in unison as Nickle looked down at the fresh stacks of crispy bills.

"If all goes well, we will have bricks for you at $12,500 a key and add 20 birds to what you asked for," Rozay said as he dapped up Nickle and Tru.

Tru imagined the meeting going okay but not this good. He couldn't believe the amount of dope they were about to get plus taking over an entire operation that was already running smoothly. They were going from small corners boys to kingpins overnight

. Part two

After a usual night of fucking two random hoes in his luxury penthouse, Procaine felt relaxed and well rested. His stomach growled just as he was pulling into Rosie Beez. He parked his truck and went to sit in his usual spot.

"Bri, I want to try something different today," he sighed.

"Okay, what would you like baby?" she responded in her deep southern drawl as she got out her small notepad to place his order.

"You know what I like; wow me," he said dismissing her from his table.

The constant buzzing of his Motorola Razr irritated him. Just as he picked up the phone, his irritation turned into rage. "If you call my muthafuckin phone again, I'mma ring your neck," he said through clenched teeth realizing this was Gisele's 9th call so far.

"I just want you to come home," she sobbed as he hung up on her.

"Where the fuck this lil nigga at, I ain't got all day," he thought to himself. His patience ran thinner as he ate his food waiting for Nickle to show up.

Outside in the parking lot, Fist pulled their van aside Procaine's Excursion as LJ and Yazzy crept out to the back door of Procaine's SUV. Once Nickle saw Fist driving away, he jogged up to the trunk to shut it and walked into Rosie Beez.

"About damn time," Procaine huffed as he wiped the syrup from the sides of his mouth with a napkin.

"If you can't be on time with ten lil bricks, how the fuck you supposed to handle more?" he joked but was dead ass serious.

"Did you bring more nigga?" Nickle asked with irritation in his tone.

"Still working on it, and each key will be $17,500," Procaine responded shortly.

"Ight then. Drive safe," Nickle retorted as he left the restaurant with a bag full of product.

"Gotta love free drugs," he chuckled to himself as he passed the drugs off to one of his workers and headed to the van with the rest of the crew waiting anxiously across the street.

When Procaine climbed into his oversized Excursion, he felt a prick and tingling sensation in his leg. He looked down and saw a small needle sticking out his leg. "What the hell!" he mumbled to himself realizing he couldn't move his arms or legs.

"Remember me?" he heard as he tried to turn his head.

His entire body was locked, and he began to silently panic. LJ appeared from the back seat and stared at Procaine coldly. Through the side of his peripheral, Procaine could see a woman with a sinister smile on her face. She looked evil and her smile sent chills down his spine.

"This serum will last an hour, but you will feel everything I promise," Yazzy said as she gave him the kiss of death on his lips.

In one swift motion, she and LJ threw his limp body into the passenger seat, and she quickly sped off. Procaine tried to yell as loud as he could, but his lips would not move. His face felt numb and frozen. He could hear the screams in his head, but his lips were too heavy to open. He tried everything to attempt to move or speak, but it was pointless because only little murmurs came from the side of his lips.

"Shut the fuck up bitch," LJ shouted as he knocked Procaine out with the butt of his pistol.

"How long before we get to Sam Houston National Forest?" he asked impatiently.

"56 minutes," she responded as she headed I45 north with the crew's van tailing not too far behind.

Sam Houston Forest was a large forest surrounded by overgrown trees, wildlife, and Lake Conroe. The forest was at least 163,000 acres and had dozens of small hiking trails. With Lake Conroe nearby, the forest was also surrounded by small creeks and rivers. It was the perfect place to get rid of Procaine because finding him would take days or months if the animals didn't get to him first.

Yazzy turned into an off-road vehicle trail and double

parked the Excursion once she was certain they were far from the road. The crew's van pulled in and circled around the Excursion to make sure they could get out the trail with Procaine's oversized SUV taking up most of the passage. Once they confirmed the path was cleared, LJ climbed out the backseat. Yazzy made sure all the doors were shut, all vents were closed, and all windows were sealed before she pulled the bomb CeCe concocted and threw it into Procaine's lap. She hopped out and ran as fast as she could to the other side of the trail where the team was all watching and wearing gas masks.

It only took two minutes for the smoke from the smoke bomb to fully engulf the large SUV. The burning sensation on his skin awoke Procaine from his unconsciousness. His body felt hot like fire, and the burning pain in his eyes blurred his vision. He could smell blood and burning flesh and his uncontrollable vomit was everywhere. The sensation in his legs were starting to come back, and he felt the urge to run. His skin was peeling, and his hair began dropping like radiation was in the air.

He could feel his heart beating through his chest as he looked down at his bloody soaked shirt. His breathing became painful, but he managed to let out an excruciating scream. His blood curling scream was the last thing you heard before the smoke cleared.

"This some real gangsta ass shit right here," Tru said in amusement.

"Damn CeCe I'm gone need more of those bombs,"

Yazzy chuckled.

Once it was safe to go back to the Excursion, LJ glanced at the skeletal remains of Procaine and asked Tiny to pass him the machete. He used the machete to hack at the remaining flesh connecting Procaine's skull to his body. With several hard hacks, Procaine's spine cracked, and his head rolled off. LJ picked up his head and punted it into the woods.

"Come back from that muthafucka!" he said as he and the crew hopped into the van and drove around the abandoned SUV.

"We are really unstoppable now," Tangela giggled with excitement as she thought about conquering Houston and the Chuck with nobody in their way.

Chapter 10: Blood Ties

The sun beams radiated on Nickle's Candy painted Caddy as his '84s spoked rims slowly turned onto Southwind St. in South Park. He double parked in front of the trap and stepped out with Tru by his side.

"Aye, who in charge?" Nickle asked a young jit passing him by. The young boy stopped and pointed to a corner boy posted on a stoop.

"Preciate it," Tru said as he handed the boy a crisp hundred-dollar bill. The corner boy stood up immediately and clutched his pistol.

"You can relax," Nickle said flashing his .45 in his pants uncocked.

"We here cuz Procaine went into early retirement. This burner phone got everything you need to know. Meet us at the address in the memo in one hour." Nickle uttered as he handed the corner boy a burner phone.

He and Tru turned to walk back to the Caddy and put Knocking Pictures Off Da Wall by YungStar on full blast. The sounds of Knocking Pictures Off Da Wall flowed through his sub-woofer speakers as Nickle and Tru nodded their heads in unison. Their presence became known almost immediately when they turned onto Liberty Rd off 59 North. This area is known as Dope Fiend Land or DFL for short. Nickle pulled alongside a dope boy who was walking up to cars and serving them. Once the dope boy got to him, he downed his passenger window.

"Procaine retired. We got the work now," Tru said. "Take this burner and meet us at the address in the memo within one hour." He repeated to the dope boy.

"Bet," the dope boy responded as he backed away from the Caddy.

Nickle turned the radio back up as he sped off to their part of Fifth Ward. "This shit better go smoothly," Tru muttered as he shifted in his seat. He didn't like dealing with new niggas, but he knew they needed workers badly.

"I don't see why this shit would go left. We giving these niggas work," Nickle replied.

"Man, them Liberty Rd niggas different," Tru said as he sucked his teeth.

"They better fall in line," he exclaimed as they rode in silence the rest of the way to BuckTown, a small section in Fifth Ward.

Almost two hours passed before the dope boys from SouthPark, and Liberty Rd pulled up. "We having safes installed at each trap." Nickle said jump starting the meeting.

"We all work as a team; no man is above the other. Each person has a code to the safes, and we split everything after we feed our teams. Nobody starve and all we ask for is loyalty," Nickle said with a serious tone.

"The more workers, the better," Tru added. "You niggas need to start recruiting. We taking on a major load now, and everybody gone eat. I promise dat!" he said with conviction.

"The burners we gave y'all, use it to reach out to us," Nickle mentioned. "We gone meet at least once a week to make sure all the traps running smoothly. If y'all need more weight, they going for fifteen a key and whatever you buy, we front the same amount. The drops will be announced every week, and the meet ups will be the same day as the drop. Any questions?" he said as he glanced the room for confirmation.

"Bet then! There shouldn't be any misunderstandings. Feed y'all team and get y'all hittas with the program." Tru said as he passed each dope boy $25,000.

The dope boys, Nickle, and Tru dapped each other up before they all headed out the trap.

"Nigga we think we Tony Montana and Manny," Tru joked as he felt a relief from the meeting.

"Scarface ain't got shit on us," Nickle chucked as he revved up his Caddy.

They pulled into the long driveway of the Westheimer Condo, and Tru sent a text to the team letting them know they were outside. Within minutes, Becky opened the door and motioned them to come in. From what Nickle could see, the team was preparing for a meeting.

"Everything good...we got all the dope boys on board,"

Nickle said as he propped onto the luxurious sectional.

"CeCe on the phone with the connect. We waiting on the location of the drop right na," Fist said putting the two on point.

"Go to We keep It Safe Storage Unit on Almeda Rd. and meet Emilio at the second storage unit when you pull in. The drop is in exactly one hour from this phone call, Cecelita." CeCe heard as Rodrigo stern demeanor intensified.

"Cecelita...come alone," he said as he disconnected the call. She placed her phone in her back pocket and rushed into the living room. She realized she had a small window of time and needed to leave ASAP.

"Y'all I gotta go alone," she said with fear all over her face.

"Nah, fuck that we ride out together," Tangela shouted.

"Y'all don't understand. It's important I follow his exact rules," CeCe retorted as she hurried out the door and into a black Denali truck.

"I'll follow her to make sure she straight if some shit pop off," Tiny said reassuring the girls. He grabbed two bullet proof vests, a semi-automatic, and two shotguns.

He headed to a Jetta and made sure CeCe was up ahead. He noticed her bending the corner and started backing his car up. He made sure to keep his distance as the ride went on for miles and miles. Up ahead, he could tell they were going into a rural area. The lanes went from a four-lane highway to a two-lane small road. He quickly realized he needed another way of tailing her without blowing his cover.

When CeCe pulled into the storage unit, she parked in front of the second unit just like she was instructed to do. Her uncle, Emilio, was surrounded by dozens of heavily armed henchmen. He motioned for her to get out and pop the trunk. On demand, CeCe hopped out and moved aside as the henchmen began loading up the trunk. She was so anxious, and her nerves were wrecked. The anxiousness was written all over her face.

"I can't wait to get back to the Chuck," she thought to herself as they loaded up the final boxes.

One of the henchmen gave Emilio a thumbs up signifying they were able to load up the Denali. "One ton of pure cocaína...Cecelita," he said as he glanced over to a terrified CeCe.

"Do you know why your mother was disowned?" he asked with amusement. CeCe stared blankly and turned to walk back to the Denali.

"She was disloyal to her own kind. That same venomous blood runs within you," he said with disgust as he followed her to the truck. "Your mother was a traitor who didn't pay la' Familia for her sins," he retorted as he snapped his fingers.

Tiny pulled over as he debated if he should blow his cover. "Better safe than sorry," he shrugged as he shifted back into drive. "What the fuck...." He mumbled as he saw three black Suburbans coming down the narrow road at full speed. He mashed the gas and attempted to outrun the three SUVs, but it was too late. One truck cut in front of him as another pulled alongside of him. Tiny reached for his pistol, downed his passenger window, and let off as many shots as he could blindly. The Suburban behind him collided with his small Jetta, and he accidentally shot the roof. The Suburban beside him shot his front passenger tire, and Tiny began spiraling out of control.

He lost control of his steering wheel and sent his car crashing into a tree. The collision imploded his airbags and almost knocked him out. His vision blurred a bit, and he could hear ringing in his ears. He tried to climb out, but his seat belt was stuck. His body was too massive to maneuver in the small, compacted Jetta. The Mexican henchmen approached his wrecked vehicle slowly. One of them used the butt of their rifle to bust out the driver's window. Before Tiny could fight back, the henchmen hit him with the same rifle and pulled out a knife and began to cut him out his seatbelt. They dragged Tiny to the backseat of the Suburban and sped off.

At the snap of Emilio's fingers, the henchmen threw Tiny out of the backseat of the SUV and onto the ground near CeCe's feet. He was gagged and tied up. His face was covered in bruises and barely recognizable.

"Tiny?" CeCe questioned in disbelief. "I told y'all I needed to go alone!" she yelled in frustration. "Why did you follow me?" she shakily asked as her eyes shifted.

She knew they were about to face severe consequences. A single tear fell from her eye as she noticed her uncle closing in on her.

"You gotta crew that don't listen I see Cecelita," he taunted. With each step, she felt smaller and smaller. She slowly backed up towards the Denali, and her mind began racing.

"How the fuck I'mma get both of us out this situation." She thought to herself as her back collided with the truck's driver door. Emilio stared at her with pure hatred as he stood over her. With one swift motion, he sliced her throat from ear-to-ear with a razor-sharp switchblade.

CeCe slid down the car as she gargled the blood pooling in her throat. Tiny felt helpless as he tried butt hopping to her. Her face became blue, and her lips were pale. Her eyes darkened, and her hand dropped from her neck. Her blood seeped into the ground as she appeared empty of life.

"Put her in the Denali," Emilio demanded as one of the henchmen threw CeCe's lifeless body into the back seat. Emilio climbed into the passenger seat and watched the henchmen combat with Tiny.

Tiny struggled to overpower the henchmen as he head butted every single one of them that came into his direction. After a small tussle, they threw him into the back of the Suburban cargo area and followed the other henchmen driving the Denali. The trucks bullied 610 as they bobbed and weaved the late evening Houston traffic.

The Suburbans lined up the curb as the Denali pulled into the driveway of the Westheimer Condo. Emilio climbed out of the Denali and into one of the Suburbans.

Once he was far enough into the distance, he sent a group text to the crew from CeCe's phone "Outside," threw the phone to the floor, and stomped on it. He tossed the small fragments of the phone out his window and chuckled to himself. "To hell you go with that traidora," he said as he upped his window and sunk into his seat.

Tangela jumped at the sound of her phone chiming. "Outside," she read as she sprinted to the door. She could see the dark Denali's driver door was wide open.

"CeCe?" she questioned as she walked to the truck.

As she got closer, she smelt the one thing she knew too well...the smell of blood. She closed the SUV door and ran inside to grab LJ and the crew with tears welled in her eyes. Becky's knees buckled once she saw CeCe. She recognized a throat slitting from afar. LJ's face turned to stone as he scooped CeCe from the backseat and carried her inside. He laid her down softly on the bed and tried to keep his composure.

"I want their heads," Yazzy shouted as she manically paced the floor.

"Let's get the dollies and go grab the boxes," Fist motioned to Rozay as they left out the condo.

Fist angrily slid the boxes across the living room as grief finally settled in. The girls were comforting each other on the couch and swearing on vengeance to soothe themselves.

"Where is Tiny?" Yazzy shrieked as she ran out to the truck.

There were no signs of his body or body parts. All the boxes were filled with Columbian cocaine. Yazzy walked back in with a note she found in the back seat of the Denali. That said, "no más lazos de sangre" or "No more blood ties." She read out loud as she balled up the paper and threw it across the room.

The constant ring tone of Tiny's phone made Tangela assume the worst. Her heart was pumping a mile a minute, and her head was spinning. She felt like she was going to faint and fell to the floor in tears. This team and her daughter were all she knew. After one more quick call, LJ gave up. His face was hot, and he was fuming.

"Let's give these fuckin' wetbacks a war." He bellowed out in frustration.

Chapter 11: Make You an Offer You Can't Refuse

Rozay dialed Nickle's phone number quickly and tapped his foot as the dial tone continued to ring.

"The work is here, and get somebody to dispose of a car," he said quickly when Nickle answered.

"Where we gone bury her?" Tangela sniffled as she wiped the tears from her eyes. CeCe had no other family, and they wouldn't dare throw a funeral not knowing when and if the Riviera Cartel would sneak them again.

"Mexico....in her mother's grave," Yazzy sighed remembering a conversation she and CeCe had a long time ago.

"If something ever happens to me, put me in the grave with my family," CeCe joked.

"Bitch, give me the blunt; you too high," Yazzy said as she laughed her off.

"I'm serious or bitch I'll haunt your ass for the rest of your life," CeCe giggled between the puffs of marijuana.

"Damn CeCe," LJ reminisced.

Leaving Texas without CeCe was too much to grasp. The team was always around death, but CeCe's death lingered and not knowing if Tiny was dead or alive made it worse. LJ was so deep into his thoughts; he barely heard his phone ringing. He looked up at the 702-area code number flashing on the screen and answered waiting for the person to speak.

"LJ..." he heard faintly.

He recognized Erika's voice immediately, and his whole body tensed up. LJ prepared himself for whatever bullshit she was about to say. He could hear constant buzzing sounds in her background, and his irritation was becoming apparent.

"LJ!!" She repeated. "I need you to know I got Lupus. All those drugs and shit that I was messing with made my condition worse. The doctors gave me a few days to live. Since I ain't gone make it much longer, I need you to know," she gasped.

"Before I go, I need you to know I wouldn't change a muthafuckin thing. Fuck you, fuck your unborn child, and fuck that bitch Sasha! I hope you die alone and miserable you bastard." She spewed as she tried to catch her breath.

After a long pause and no response from LJ, she disconnected the call feeling accomplished. When LJ got the call days later that she passed away, it didn't faze him. He felt like he had bigger shit to worry about. Finding Tiny became priority number one. The whole team was ready to get the fuck outta Texas. The longer they were there, the worse they felt. It felt like the whole state was bad luck.

Everybody began working around the clock. They needed to break into the Riviera Ranch and locate Tiny.

This became more difficult than they expected because they weren't sure Tiny, Rodrigo, or Emilio was there. They weren't willing to put all their lives in danger, and the whole plan was uncertain. Rozay called the one person indebted to him for life...Salvador.

Sal was a dirty cop turned private investigator from Philly, and he was on Rozay's payroll. Sal did so much fucked up and grimy shit to the point Rozay had to protect him from street niggas. Rozay owned Sal, and he moved whenever Rozay said so.

"Sal, get to Houston a fuckin' sap. I got some shit for you to do," he said once Sal answered.

When Sal arrived later that evening, Rozay gave him the rundown on Tiny. Even though Rozay knew Sal was indebted to him, he never gave him too much information. He felt like once a cop, always a cop, dirty or not.

"This one of my peoples' little brother, and he went missing a couple of days ago. Find out his last whereabouts, and get back to me," Rozay demanded as Sal began jotting down Tiny's full name, description, and vehicle information.

"I'll get on it right away," Sal said confidently as he scurried out of the condo.

Early the next morning, Sal called Rozay and requested they meet up somewhere. The entire crew loaded up in two Expeditions and headed to a restaurant called The Cadillac Bar. Sal was already seated when they arrived.

"What you got for us?" Rozay said anxiously.

Sal cleared his throat and responded "The car information you gave me was found abandoned two days ago by HPD. The driver's side window was busted out, and the driver's side seatbelt was cut. I'm not sure if he escaped or not, but there aren't any bodies in the morgue that matches his description, and no recent hospital entries with his description either. He may still be out there somewhere."

"Man shit, Tiny where the fuck you at ma nigga?" LJ muttered in Geechie as Tangela lowered her head.

"You can go," Rozay said as he dismissed Sal.

"We need to get back home and figure this shit out," Becky said impatiently.

"After we bury CeCe," Yazzy said with a serious look on her face.

"How we gone get her body across the border?" Tangela gasped realizing they must travel with her dead body.

"Let me make a call to Sal and find out where her mom and pops buried at, and I'll get us a private jet to Mexico," Rozay said putting the plans together.

"You think Sal can get us the information by tonight?" LJ asked Rozay.

"Hell yeah!" Rozay responded.

Just as expected, Sal was able to locate the graves of

CeCe's parents at a small gravesite in Tijuana, Mexico. Since Texas bordered with Mexico, the flight was only 3 hours, 5 minutes. Before their flight at 6 pm, they dropped 200 kilos of cocaine off to Nickle and packed the rest of boxes to take to Charleston. They made sure to wipe everything down in the condo as they prepared to go back to Charleston after their quick trip to Mexico. As badly as Yazzy didn't want to, she folded CeCe into a large garment bag and they gently laid her into the oversized trunk of the Fleetwood Cadillac Fist stole from a parking garage.

The ride to the field where the jet landed was heavy, and no one spoke. When they arrived, it took almost an hour to load up the jet with all the boxes of coke, their luggage, and CeCe. Tangela wiped everything down before she lit a match. The Cadillac went up in flames and burned any evidence of them being attached to it. The private jet took off into the sky and landed with ease at Tijuana International Airport. Thanks to Marcus' connections in Mexico, they were able to secure two small rental cars without using any identification.

They wasted no time driving to the cemetery that was at least two hours away. When they arrived, chills settled down their spine. The cemetery was small, dark, and ominous. Wild animals roamed the site freely, and the darkness overcame the sky. The only light was moonlight, and it made it impossible to walk around the cemetery without stepping on graves. The team spread out as they flashed each grave with a flashlight.

"Found them!" Becky said as she read the names

Guillermo and Valentina De León.

"Who should we bury her with?" Tangela asked as she glanced over the graves.

"Her mama," Yazzy said as she began digging.

Becky and Tangela held the lights as Rozay, LJ, Yazzy, and Fist dug furiously into the hollow grave. Yazzy prayed for forgiveness as she shifted up the dirt. They could see the shine on Valentina's coffin and began digging faster. Once the hole was big enough, LJ kneeled and grabbed the garment bag containing CeCe's decayed body. He threw her into the unearthed grave and began covering her in dirt. As they covered her, each one of them said their final goodbyes silently.

The team circled around the grave to make sure it looked untouched and walked back to their cars. They wasted no time getting back on their jet as they prepared for the long six-hour flight back to South Carolina. Everyone began to doze off as LJ stayed up in his thoughts. He wanted to bring the whole Riviera Cartel down. He was tired of the drug shit, tired of constantly being at war, but he knew he would always have to look over his shoulders if he didn't kill Rodrigo and Emilio himself.

When they arrived in Charleston, it felt like a breath of fresh air. The familiar smell of the paper mill in the air, the palmetto trees danced in the breeze, and the sky was blue with no clouds in sight. It almost felt like paradise.

"Home sweet home," Becky shrieked.

Before they could enjoy the moment, everyone's phone chimed as they read the text.

"I see that y'all made it back safe and in good health. Have the payment for shipment in full by next Tuesday."

A second text chimed. "If you want to see your amigo alive again."

"How the fuck we supposed to get rid of over 900 plus kilos in one week?" Fist asked with astonishment.

"These Mexicans ain't playing fair at all," Rozay chimed in thinking about the fucked-up circumstances.

"We gotta do this shit for Tiny and CeCe," Yazzy added.

Tangela looked over to LJ, "I know you don't want anything to do with this dope shit LJ, but we gone need you. Are you in or out...?"

THE END

Follow @BIANCHI_BRAND on Instagram

Add Don Bianchi on Facebook

Made in the USA
Columbia, SC
08 February 2025

53463301R00057